THAT
DOGGONE DOG

by Alison Strickland
illustrated by Don Robison

Fourth printing by Willowisp Press 1997.

Published by Willowisp Press
801 94th Avenue North, St. Petersburg, Florida 33702

Printed in the United States of America

4 6 8 10 9 7 5

ISBN 0-87406-300-0

This book is dedicated to my husband . . .
and to happy endings.

1

Ted squirmed at his desk and checked the clock. It can't be five more minutes until the bell rings, he thought. That clock must be stuck. Ted started to think about the weekend. When the bell rang at last, Ted jumped.

"You may go now, boys and girls," the teacher said. Ted hurried out of the classroom and out the school door. He was ready to burst with excitement. As soon as he got past the crossing guard, he began to run.

"Here, Buttons! Come here, girl!" Ted called as he turned the corner of his street.

The big dalmatian sat by the driveway that led into Ted's house. When she heard him call, she leaped to her feet. Then she loped down the sidewalk toward him. When they met, Buttons jumped up and put her big paws on Ted's shoulders. Her long, wet tongue licked his face.

"Good old Buttons. How come you always know when I'm coming home from school? Huh?" Ted asked.

Ted pushed Buttons away. "Now, sit," he ordered. But the dalmatian wiggled her tail with joy. "Looks like you don't feel like sitting any more than I do." Ted laughed.

Buttons looked up at Ted and cocked her head. She looked like she was thinking about what he was saying. Ted could remember the day he and his younger brother, Bob, got Buttons. The first time Ted spoke to her, she'd cocked her head just like that. As a little puppy, she had looked like a stuffed animal with black buttons sewn all over her fur. That's why Ted and Bob had named her Buttons.

"Hey, Buttons, do you know that it's Friday?" Ted asked. Buttons hopped to her feet and started wiggling again. "I guess you do! Okay, girl. Let's get moving! We're going to play ball."

 **2**

"Will's coming over in just a few minutes," Ted's mother called from the hall.

"Great," Ted said. Will was his favorite kid-sitter. That's what he called himself—a kid-sitter. Will said guys like Ted and Bob were too big for baby-sitters. They really liked Will. He always thought up fun things for them to do.

"Wow, you sure are dressed up," Ted said as his mother walked into the room. She was wearing a shiny green dress. She was carrying a feathery hat. Ted's dad had given her the hat for Christmas. She always wore it when she was going some-place special.

"We're going to Dad's company party," she said. "It's at the big hotel downtown. I'll leave the telephone number for you." She put the hat down on the couch. Then she walked over to the desk and began writing.

Buttons came into the den. Suddenly, the big dog stopped and stared at the couch. Then she growled softly. Before anyone could stop her, Buttons leaped onto the couch. She took the hat in her mouth and started to shake it. Feathers flew everywhere.

"Oh, no!" Ted's mother yelled. "Get it away from her. Ted, stop her!"

Ted ran to Buttons. He grabbed the hat and pulled. "Buttons, let go!" he yelled. But Buttons didn't let go. She only pulled harder. The hat ripped in two.

"Bad dog!" Ted's mother yelled. "Look what you've done! My hat is ruined. You boys get that doggone dog out of here!"

"I'll bet your mother was furious," Will said. He was helping Ted and Bob pick up feathers.

"She was pretty mad," Ted answered. "She yelled at Buttons and made us put her outside. Then she told us to clean up the mess. After that, she and Dad left."

"It wasn't Buttons' fault," Bob said. "Buttons thought the hat was a bird. She was only following her instincts."

"I think that's all the feathers," Will said. "Should we let the criminal back in?"

Bob ran and opened the back door. Buttons came slinking inside. She didn't look at anyone. She went into the den and hid underneath the grand piano.

"She sure looks guilty," Will said.

"That's where she always hides when she gets into trouble," Ted said.

"I have an idea," Will said. "Let's cheer her up. Let's teach Buttons to play hide-and-seek."

"Dogs don't play hide-and-seek," Bob said seriously.

"I'll bet Buttons could learn," Ted answered.

"Yeah, but first we have to get her to come out from under the piano," Will said.

Ted called Buttons. Buttons wouldn't budge. She just looked at them with her sad eyes.

"I know," Bob said. "I'll get some dog biscuits. Then she'll come out."

When Buttons saw the biscuits, she wagged her tail. But she didn't come out.

"Buttons, you are a good girl," Ted called to her.

"Yeah, we're not mad at you," Bob told her.

Finally Buttons crawled out.

"Get her ball," Will said. "We'll throw the ball down the steps. When she runs to get it, we'll all hide. She'll get the ball. Then she'll start looking for us. The first time, we'll all hide in the same place. When she gets the idea, we can hide in different places."

"Go get the ball, Buttons," Ted said as he tossed it down the stairs. Buttons scampered after the ball. The three boys ran and hid in the shower.

They heard Buttons running up the stairs. She started barking. Then she looked in each boy's room. When she couldn't find them, she barked again. Bob giggled. Buttons ran into the bathroom. She pushed the shower curtain with her nose. When she saw the boys, she ran and got her ball. Then she ran back and dropped it in front of them.

The boys played hide-and-seek with Buttons for a long time. She learned to find them when they hid in different places.

"See, I told you she could learn to play hide-and-seek," Ted said. "Buttons is about the smartest dog in the world."

4

That night, Ted couldn't get to sleep. He started thinking about what he was going to do.

The more Ted thought about what he would do, the more wide awake he felt.

Cookies, he thought. Cookies and milk would make me sleepy.

He started down the stairs toward the kitchen. Then he heard his father's voice.

"I know it will be hard for the boys in the beginning, Margie. But they'll get over it," he said.

Ted stopped on the stairs. *Hard for the boys.* What does Dad mean? Ted wondered.

I shouldn't be listening, he thought. I feel like I'm spying. Still, he couldn't seem to move.

"I know they'll get over it," his mother said. "But it makes me sad to think about the kids having to move again. We've only been here two years. They've just started to feel really at home."

"At least they can stay here until after school's out," his dad said. "I have to start working in the new office next week. But I'll come home every weekend until we move."

"Move?" Ted whispered aloud. "I don't want to move. This is home. I belong here."

Ted couldn't stand to listen anymore.

He tiptoed up the stairs. When he got to Bob's room, he stopped. He eased open the door.

"Here, Buttons," he called softly.

He heard Buttons jump off Bob's bed. He hoped Bob didn't wake up. He opened the door wide enough for Buttons to get out.

Buttons followed Ted into his room. Ted sat on the edge of the bed. He felt like crying. Buttons sat at Ted's feet and put her head on his knees. She looked up at him and whined.

"You always understand, don't you, girl?" Ted said. He stroked Buttons' head and rubbed her ears.

"If we have to move, at least I'll still have you, Buttons." Ted sighed.

"Boys, your mother and I need to talk to you about something," Ted's dad said.

Ted and his family were eating breakfast. He'd just taken a bite of toast. Here comes the bad news, he thought. His throat got dry. He felt like he might choke.

"I have a new job with my company. It's a better job," Ted's dad said.

Ted stared at his plate. Bob didn't say anything.

"I know it will be hard to go," their mother said. "Dad and I hate for you both to have to leave your friends."

Ted glanced up. His mother looked sad. He wanted to cheer her up.

"It's okay," he said. "We'll find new friends. Anyway, we'll still have Buttons to play with."

His mother's face got even sadder. She glanced nervously at his dad.

"I'm really sorry, boys," Ted's dad said. "Buttons can't go with us."

Hot tears came to Ted's eyes. "You can't make us move without Buttons!" he cried. "It's because she tore up Mother's hat, isn't it? Buttons will never do anything like that again. I promise!"

"No, Ted," his dad said gently. "It has nothing to do with the hat. We're going to be living in the city. We'd have to keep her on a leash all the time. She'd hate that."

"She'd hate not being with us more than being on a leash," Bob said.

"I'm sure she'll be upset for a few days," his dad said. "But she'll get used to her new home."

"What new home?" Ted asked. "Where would she live?"

"Mrs. Fisher wants her," Ted's mother said. "Buttons is fine with her when we go away. It's not like we have to leave her with strangers. She'll just be moving next door."

"Mrs. Fisher won't play with her like we do. Buttons is a kid's dog. Buttons loves to play," Ted argued.

"Buttons will be a watchdog. Mr. Fisher travels a lot. With Buttons there, Mrs. Fisher won't be so nervous being in the house alone at night," his mother said.

"I'm really sorry, guys," their dad said. "There's just no other way."

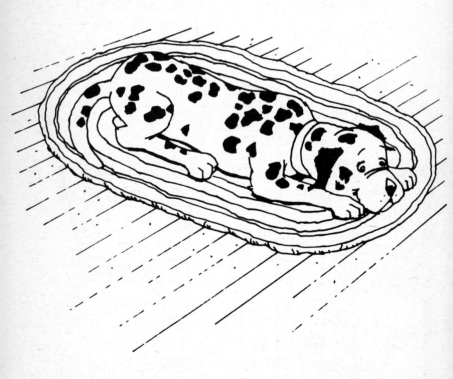

 **6**

The last few weeks of school flew by. Moving day came quickly for Ted.

"You'd better take Buttons over to Mrs. Fisher now," Ted's dad said. "The moving van will be here soon. She'll get upset if she sees the furniture going out."

"Do you want me to take her over?" the boys' mother asked.

"Bob and I will do it," Ted said, sighing.

Ted got the leash and went to get the dog. "You bring her dish and her food, Bob," he said softly.

Ted and Bob walked slowly to the Fishers' house. Mrs. Fisher was waiting for them.

"I'll take good care of her, guys," Mrs. Fisher said.

Ted didn't say anything. He was afraid he was going to cry. He looked at Bob. Bob's lower lip was trembling.

"Thanks," Ted whispered. He turned and ran. He didn't want to say good-bye to Buttons. If I don't tell her good-bye, maybe she won't know I'm gone, he thought.

7

Ted and Bob liked their new apartment. It was near a city park with lots of playing fields. They met new friends. But they missed Buttons a lot. Ted and Bob wrote Buttons a letter. They knew it was a silly thing to do. But it made them feel better.

A year passed, then another. Then on Ted's birthday, he got a surprise. His dad got another promotion. They were moving again. But this time it was different. The new job was in their old hometown . . . the town where Buttons was.

 **8**

"I still don't understand why we can't get Buttons back," Ted said.

"That wouldn't be fair," his dad said. "You can't give someone a dog and take it back two years later. Besides, Buttons might not even know you."

"No, Dad," Ted answered. "Buttons will always remember us."

"Sure she will," his mother replied.
"Could we go see Buttons?" Bob asked.

"Of course. Our new house is only a few miles from the Fishers. After we get all settled in, we'll go over for a visit," his mother said.

"Can we take our bikes and explore the new neighborhood now?" Ted asked.

"Sure," his dad said.

"Just don't go too far," his mother said.

The boys rode off. They found a lake where they could fish. Then they decided to ride further. They wanted to find a ball field.

"Hey, Bob," Ted called as they pedaled around a corner. "Isn't that the street that ran in front of our old school? This is starting to look really familiar. I'll bet we could find our old house from here. Then we could find Buttons, too."

"Mother said our old house was three or four miles away. We'd get into trouble if we went that far," Bob said.

"Well, we haven't gone too far yet. Let's just see where this takes us," Ted said.

Soon Ted spotted their old school in the distance. "There's the school, Bob. See? Way down the street. Our old house is just a few blocks from that school," he said.

"Yeah, but the school is across a four-lane street. A really busy four-lane street," Bob said.

Ted knew he shouldn't cross the street. He also knew Buttons was nearby. He wanted to go find Buttons.

"Look, Bob, there's a stoplight," Ted called when they got to the corner. "This isn't a dangerous place to cross. Let's go." The boys rode across the street.

"There's our old house," Ted said. "Look how small the tree in the front yard is. I used to think that tree was huge!"

"That's because we're bigger," Bob said. "Compared to us, the tree doesn't seem as big as it used to."

"Is that the Fishers' place?" Bob asked. He pointed to a house surrounded by a chain-link fence.

"Yeah, but they didn't have that fence. Let's go see if we can find Buttons," Ted said.

 **9**

"Hey, you guys, don't go in there! A really mean dog lives in there."

Ted and Bob turned around. A couple of boys were walking toward them.

"What's the dog look like?" Ted asked.

"It's white with black spots. It's really, really big."

"That's Buttons," Ted told Bob.

Ted and Bob went up to the fence and looked through the chain links. Then they heard a dog barking. The bark was deep and loud. It sounded mean.

What if she doesn't remember us? Ted thought. What if it's not Buttons? What if it's a mean dog that doesn't know us?

The dog ran around the corner. It snarled and bared its teeth. It looked like it was going to attack them.

"Look out, you guys!" the kids yelled.

Ted was ready to jump back. Suddenly the dog stopped and sniffed the air.

"Come here, Buttons," Ted called. "You remember us. It's Ted and Bob."

The dog cocked her head. Then her tail began to wag. In an instant the dog ran to them. Buttons began to lick their faces through the fence.

The kids from the neighborhood watched. "How did you do that?" one asked. "Every time we go near the fence, that dog acts like it's going to eat us alive."

"We're famous animal tamers." Ted laughed.

10

When Ted and Bob got home, their mother was fixing lunch. "Mrs. Fisher called while you were gone," she said. "We had an interesting talk."

Ted couldn't tell if their mother was angry.

"I know we weren't supposed to go over to the Fishers' house," Ted said. "But pretty soon we were almost there. We just wanted to see Buttons."

"I know you did," his mother said. "But both your dad and I told you not to ride that far. When Dad gets home, we need to talk over some things."

But when Ted's dad got home, no one mentioned a family conference.

Then at Sunday breakfast, Ted's dad said, "I understand you fellows have been to see Buttons. Is that right?"

"I'm sorry, I just—" Ted started.

His dad interrupted him. "I hear old Buttons was really glad to see you two."

"We've had a long talk with Mrs. Fisher," his mother said. "It seems that after we moved, Buttons kept going to our old house. She'd even run away to the park. Buttons seemed to be looking for you. The Fishers had to put up the fence to keep her home."

"I told you so," Ted said. "I told you she was a kid's dog."

"Looks like you were right," his dad answered. "After they put up the fence, Buttons started barking and growling a lot."

Then his mother said, "Mrs. Fisher told us Buttons had been going to the door and whining ever since you boys were there. She thinks Buttons would be a lot happier with us."

"Please, can we get Buttons back?" Ted asked hopefully.

The boys' parents looked at each other and smiled.

"Under one condition," their dad said. "You have to teach Buttons the difference between a hat and a bird!"

That afternoon Ted and Bob's dad took them to get Buttons. Ted and Bob put her in the backseat with them. Buttons wouldn't sit still. During the ride home, she licked their faces. She even licked their dad's ears as he drove.

When they got home, Buttons started up the front steps. Then she stopped. Ted's dad's old straw fishing hat sat on a porch chair. Fishing flies stuck out of the hatband. The flies were made of feathers.

Suddenly Buttons ran for the hat. She bit the brim and started shaking it. "Let go, Buttons!" Ted yelled. He was afraid that Buttons would cut herself on the fishhooks. He was also afraid that his dad would be really angry.

Ted grabbed for the hat. "Give me that, Buttons," he yelled. "You've only been home a minute, and you're in trouble!"

Buttons let go of the hat. She had torn a big hole in the brim. Ted turned and gave the hat to his dad. "I can fix that," Ted said.

"It's okay, son." Then Ted's dad smiled at his wife. "Looks like we're even now. We've both lost a hat to Buttons," he said.

"At least she's proved that she hasn't changed!" Bob said. "She's still that doggone dog."

"Yup, there's no doubt about it." Ted laughed with relief. "She is the same old Buttons. And Buttons is home!"